TRUDEL'S SIEGE

TRUDEL'S SIEGE

LOUISA MAY ALCOTT

ART BY STAN SKARDINSKI

McGraw-Hill Book Company
New York St. Louis San Francisco Auckland Düsseldorf Johannesburg Kuala Lumpur London Mexico Montreal New Delhi Panama Paris São Paulo Singapore Sydney Tokyo Toronto

Library of Congress Cataloging in Publication Data

Main entry under title:

Trudel's siege.

SUMMARY: Trudel helps her family through hunger and sickness by giving up her one treasure, thus beginning a cycle of beneficial events.
I. Alcott, Louisa May, 1832-1888. Trudel's siege. II.Skardinski,Stan.
PZ7.T7764 [E] 76-3405
ISBN 0-07-057791-9
ISBN 0-07-057792-7 lib. bdg.

234567 MUBP 789876

·ART FOR·
JKL
P.K. · A.C.

This book has been set in Garamond *Linofilm,* and set by Black Dot, Inc., printed by Murray Printing Co., and bound at The Book Press. The design, binding, and display face are in keeping with the period of the illustrations.

TRUDEL'S SIEGE, a story from *Lulu's Library,* has been edited, and all places and titles given their proper Dutch meaning. Miss Alcott's original story contained numerous German names and idioms.

I must thank Grosset & Dunlap Publishers, the original publishers of *Lulu's Library,* for their help in making this book possible. Some thanks also goes to Little, Brown and Company for their help. Finally, to Eleanor Nichols and Jean Sepanski at McGraw-Hill, for their trust and encouragement—all things being very ambiguous until the very end.

Stan Skardinski

GRANDMOTHER, WHAT IS THIS CURIOUS PICTURE about?" said little Gertrude, or "Trudel," as they called her, looking up from the red book that lay on her knee, one Sunday morning, when she and the grandmother sat sadly together in the neat kitchen; for the father was very ill, and the poor mother seldom left him.

The old woman put on her round spectacles, which made her look as wise as an owl, and turned to answer the child, who had been as quiet as a mouse for a long time, looking at the strange pictures in the ancient book.

"Ah, my dear, that tells about a very famous and glorious thing that happened long ago at the siege of Leiden. You can read it for yourself someday."

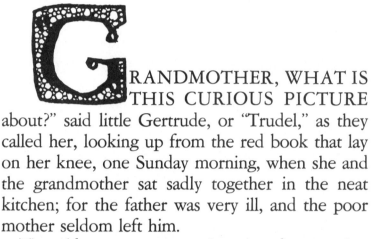

"Please tell me now. Why are the houses half under water, and ships sailing among them, and people leaning over the walls of the city? And why is that boy waving his hands on the tower, where the men are running away in a great smoke?" asked Trudel, too curious to wait till she could read the long hard words on the yellow pages.

"Well, dear, this is the story: and you shall hear how brave men and women, and children, too, were in those days. The cruel Spaniards came and besieged the city for many months; but the faithful people would not give up, though nearly starved to death. When all the bread and meat were gone and the gardens empty, they ate grass and herbs and horses, and even dogs and cats, trying to hold out till help came to them."

"Did little girls really eat their kitties? Oh, I'd die before I would kill my dear Jan," cried Trudel, hugging the pretty kitten that purred in her lap.

"Yes, the children ate their pets. And so would you if it would save your father or mother from starving. *We* know what hunger is; but we won't eat Jan yet."

The old woman sighed as she glanced from the empty table to the hearth where no fire burned.

"*Did* help come in the ships?" asked the child, bending her face over the book to hide the tears that filled her eyes, for she was very hungry, and had had only a crust for breakfast.

"Our good Prince of Orange was trying to help them; but the Spaniards were all around the city and he had not men enough to fight them by land, so he sent carrier doves with letters to tell the people that he was going to cut through the great dikes that kept the sea out, and let the water flow over the country so as to drive the enemy from his camp, for the city stood upon high ground, and would be safe. Then the ships, with food, could sail over the drowned land and save the brave people."

"Oh, I'm glad! I'm glad! These are the bad Spaniards running away, and these are poor people stretching out their hands for the bread. But what is the boy doing, in the funny tower where the wall has tumbled down?" cried Trudel, much excited.

"The smoke of burning houses rose between the city and the port so the people could not see that the Spaniards had run away; and they were afraid the ships could not get safely by. But a boy who was scrambling about, as boys always are wherever there is danger, fire, and fighting, saw the enemy go, and ran to the deserted tower to shout and

beckon to the ships to come on at once—for the wind had changed and soon the tide would flow back and leave them stranded."

"Nice boy! I wish I had been there to see him and help the poor people," said Trudel, patting the funny little figure sticking out of the pepper-pot tower like a jack-in-the-box.

"If children keep their wits about them and are brave, they can always help in some way, my dear. We don't have such dreadful wars now; but the dear God knows we have troubles enough, and need all our courage and faith to be patient in times like these"; and the grandmother folded her thin hands with another sigh, as she thought of her poor son dying for want of a few comforts, after working long and faithfully for a hard master who never came to offer any help, though a very rich man.

"Did they eat the carrier doves?" asked Trudel, still intent on the story.

"No, child; they fed and cared for them while they lived, and when they died, stuffed and set them up in the Stadhuis, so grateful were the brave burghers for the good news the dear birds brought."

"That is the best part of all. I like that story very much!" And Trudel turned the pages to find another, little dreaming what a carrier dove she herself was soon to become.

Poor Hans Dort and his family were nearly as distressed as the besieged people of Leiden, for poverty stood at the door, hunger and sickness were within, and no ship was anywhere seen coming to bring help. The father, who was a linen weaver, could no longer work in the great factory; the mother, who was a lacemaker, had to leave her work to nurse him; and the old woman could earn only a trifle by her knitting, being lame and feeble. Little Trudel did what she could—sold the stockings to get bread and medicine, picked up wood for the fire, gathered herbs for the poor soup, and ran errands for the market women, who paid her with unsalable fruit, withered vegetables, and now and then a bit of meat.

But market day came but once a week; and it was very hard to find food for the hungry mouths meantime. The Dorts were too proud to beg, so they suffered in silence, praying that help would come before it was too late to save the sick and old.

13

No other picture in the quaint book interested Trudel so much as that of the siege of Leiden; and she went back to it, thinking over the story till hunger made her look about for something to eat as eagerly as the poor starving burghers.

"Here, child, is a good crust. It is too hard for me. I kept it for you; it's the last except that bit for your mother," said the old woman, pulling a dry crust from her jacket with a smile; for though starving herself, the brave old soul thought only of her darling.

Trudel's little white teeth gnawed savagely at the hard bread, and Jan ate the crumbs as if he, too needed food. As she saw him purring about her feet, there came into the child's head a sudden idea, born of the brave story and of the cares that made her old before her time.

"Poor Jan gets thinner and thinner every day. If we are to eat him, we must do it soon, or he will not be worth cooking," she said with a curious look on the face that used to be so round and rosy, and now was white, thin, and anxious.

"Bless the child! We won't eat the poor beast! But it would be kind to give him away to someone who could feed him well. Go now, dear, and get a jug of fresh water. The father will need it, and so will you, for the crust is a dry dinner for my darling."

As she spoke, the old woman held the little girl close for a minute; and Trudel clung to her silently, finding the help she needed for her sacrifice in the love and the example grandma gave her.

Then she ran away, with the brown jug in one hand, the pretty kitten on her arm, and courage in her little heart. It was a poor neighborhood where the weavers and lacemakers lived; but nearly everyone had a good dinner on Sunday, and on her way to the fountain Trudel saw many well-spread tables, smelled the good soup in many kettles, and looked enviously at the plump children sitting quietly on the doorsteps in round caps and wooden shoes, waiting to be called in to eat of the big loaves, the brown sausages, and the cabbage soup smoking on the hearth.

When she came to the baker's house, her heart began to beat; and she hugged Jan so close it was well he was thin, or he would have mewed under the tender farewell squeezes his little mistress gave him. With a timid hand Trudel knocked, and then went in to find Vrouw Hertz and the five boys and girls at table, with good roast meat and bread and cheese and beer before them.

"Oh, the dear cat! The pretty cat! Let me pat

him! Hear him mew, and see his soft white coat," cried the children, before Trudel could speak, for they admired the snow-white kitten very much, and had often begged for it.

Trudel had made up her mind to give up to them at last her one treasure; but she wished to be paid for it, and was bound to tell her plan. Jan helped her, for smelling the meat, he leaped from her arms to the table and began to gnaw a bone on Dirck's plate, which so amused the young people that they did not hear Trudel say to their mother in a low voice, with red cheeks and beseeching eyes:

"Dear Vrouw Hertz, the father is very ill; the mother cannot work at her lace in the dark room; and grandma makes but little by knitting, though I help all I can. We have no food; can you give me a loaf of bread in exchange for Jan? I have nothing else to sell, and the children want him much."

Trudel's eyes were full and her lips trembled, as she ended with a look that went straight to stout Mother Hertz's kind heart, and told the whole sad story.

"Bless the dear child! Indeed, yes; a loaf and welcome; and see here, a good sausage also. Brenda, go fill the jug with milk. It is excellent for the sick man. As for the cat, let it stay awhile and get fat, then we will see. It is a pretty beast and worth many loaves of bread; so come again, Trudel, and do not suffer hunger while I have much bread."

As the kind woman spoke, she had bustled about, and before Trudel could get her breath, a big loaf, a long sausage, and a jug of fresh milk were in her apron and hands, and a motherly kiss made the gifts all the easier to take. Returning it heartily, and telling the children to be kind to Jan, she hastened home to burst into the quiet room, crying joyfully:

"See, grandmother, here is food—all mine. I bought it! Come, come, and eat!"

"Now, dear Heaven, what do I see? Where did the blessed bread come from?" asked the old woman, hugging the big loaf, and eying the sausage with such hunger in her face that Trudel ran for the knife and cup, and held a draft of fresh milk to her grandmother's lips before she could answer a single question.

"Stay, child, let us give thanks before we eat. Never was food more welcome or hearts more

18 grateful"; and folding her hands, the pious old woman blessed the meal that seemed to fall from heaven on that bare table. Then Trudel cut the crusty slice for herself, a large soft one for grandmother, with a good bit of sausage, and refilled the cup. Another portion and cup went upstairs to mother, whom she found asleep, with the father's hot hand in hers. So leaving the surprise for her waking, Trudel crept down to eat her own dinner, as hungry as a little wolf, amusing herself with making the old woman guess where and how she got this fine feast.

"This is our siege, grandmother; and we are eating Jan," she said at last, with the merriest laugh she had given for weeks.

"Eating Jan?" cried the old woman, staring at the sausage, as if for a moment she feared the kitten had been turned into that welcome shape by some miracle. Still laughing, Trudel told her story, and was well rewarded for her childish sacrifice by the look in grandmother's face as she said with a tender kiss:

"Thou art a carrier dove, my darling, coming home with good news and comfort under thy wing.

God bless thee, my brave little heart, and grant that our siege be not a long one before help comes to us!"

Such a happy feast! And for dessert more kisses and praises for Trudel when the mother came down to hear the story and to tell how eagerly father had drunk the fresh milk and gone to sleep again. Trudel was very well pleased with her bargain; but at night she missed Jan's soft purr for her lullaby, and cried herself to sleep, grieving for her lost pet, being only a child, after all, though trying to be a brave little woman for the sake of those she loved.

The big loaf and sausage took them nicely through the next day; but by Tuesday only crusts remained, and sorrel soup, slightly flavored with the last scrap of sausage, was all they had to eat.

On Wednesday morning, Trudel had plaited her long yellow braids with care, smoothed down her one blue skirt, and put on her little black silk cap, making ready for the day's work. She was weak and hungry, but showed a bright face as she took her old basket and said:

"Now I am off to market, grandmother, to sell

the hose and get medicine and milk for father. I shall try to pick up something for dinner. The good neighbors often let me run errands for them, and give me a kuchen, a bit of cheese, or a taste of their nice coffee. I will bring you something, and come as soon as I can."

The old woman nodded and smiled, as she scoured the empty kettle till it shone, and watched the little figure trudge away with the big empty basket, and, she knew, with a still emptier little stomach. "Coffee!" sighed the grandmother. "One sip of the blessed drink would put life into me. When shall I ever taste it again?" And the poor soul sat down to her knitting with hands that trembled from weakness.

The Het Plein was a busy and a noisy scene when Trudel arrived, for the thrifty Dutchwomen were early afoot; and stalls, carts, baskets, and cans were already arranged to make the most attractive display of fruit, vegetables, fish, cheese, butter, eggs, milk, and poultry, and the small wares country people came to buy.

Nodding and smiling, Trudel made her way through the bustle to the booth where old Vrouw

Schmidt bought and sold the blue woolen hose that adorned the stout legs of young and old.

"Good morning, child! I am glad to see thee and thy well-knit stockings, for I have orders for three pairs, and promised thy grandmother's, they are always so excellent," said the rosy-faced woman, as Trudel approached.

"I have but one pair. We had no money to buy more yarn. Father is so ill mother cannot work; and medicines cost a deal," said the child, with her large hungry eyes fixed on the breakfast the old woman was about to eat, first having made ready for the business of the day.

"See, then, I shall give thee the yarn and wait for the hose; I can trust thee, and shall ask a good price for the good work. Thou too wilt have the fever, I'm afraid! So pale and thin, poor child! Here, drink from my cup, and take a bite of bread and cheese. The morning air makes one hungry."

Trudel eagerly accepted the "sup" and the "bite," and felt new strength flow into her as the warm draft and good brown bread went down her throat.

"So many thanks! I had no breakfast. I came to see if I could get any errands here today, for I want to earn a bit if I can," she said with a sigh of satisfaction, as she slipped half of her generous slice and a good bit of cheese into her basket, regretting that the coffee could not be shared also.

As if to answer her wish, a loud cry from fat Mother Kinkle, the fishwife, rose at that moment, for a thievish cur had run off with a fish from her stall, while she gossiped with a neighbor.

Down went Trudel's basket, and away went Trudel's wooden shoes clattering over the stones while she raced after the dog, dodging in and out among the stalls till she cornered the thief under Gretchen Horn's milk cart; for at sight of the big dog who drew the four copper cans, the cur lost heart and dropped the fish and ran away.

"Well done!" said buxom Gretchen, when Trudel caught up the rescued treasure a good deal the worse for the dog's teeth and the dust it had been dragged through.

All the market women laughed as the little girl came back proudly bearing the fish, for the race had amused them. But Mother Kinkle said with a sigh, when she saw the damage done her property:

"It is spoiled; no one will buy that torn, dirty

thing. Throw it on the muckpile, child; your trouble was in vain, though I thank you for it."

"Give it to me, please, if you don't want it. We can eat it, and would be glad of it at home," cried Trudel, hugging the slippery fish with joy, for she saw a dinner in it, and felt that her run was well paid.

"Take it, then, and be off; I see Vrouw van Decken's cook coming, and you are in the way," answered the old woman, who was not a very amiable person, as everyone knew.

"That's a fine reward to make a child for running the breath out of her body for you," said Dame Troost, the handsome farm wife who sat close by among her fruit and vegetables, as fresh as her cabbages, and as rosy as her cherries.

"Better it, then, and give her a feast fit for a burgomaster. *You* can afford it," growled Mother Kinkle, turning her back on the other woman in a huff.

"That I will, for very shame at such meanness! Here, child, take these for thy fish stew, and these for thy little self," said the kind soul, throwing half a dozen potatoes and onions into the basket, and

handing Trudel a cabbage leaf full of cherries.

A happy girl was our little housewife on her way home, when the milk and medicine and loaf of bread were bought; and a comfortable dinner was quickly cooked and gratefully eaten in Dort's poor house that day.

"Surely the saints must help you, child, and open people's hearts to our need; for you come back each day with food for us, like the ravens to the people in the wilderness," said the grandmother when they sat at table.

"If they do, it is because you pray to them so heartily, mother. But I think the sweet ways and thin face of my Trudel do much to win kindness, and the good God makes her our little house-mother, while I must sit idle," answered Vrouw Dort; and she filled the child's platter again that she, at least, might have enough.

"I like it!" cried Trudel, munching an onion with her bread, while her eyes shone and a pretty color came into her cheeks. "I feel so old and brave now, so glad to help; and things happen, and I keep thinking what I will do next to get food. It's like the birds out yonder in the hedge, trying to feed their little ones. I fly up and down, pick and scratch, get a bit here and a bit there, and then my dear *old* birds have food to eat."

It really was very much as Trudel said, for her small wits were getting very sharp with these new cares; she lay awake that night trying to plan how she should provide the next day's food for her family.

"Where now, thou dear little mother bird?" asked the "Grootmoeder" next morning, when the child had washed the last dish, and was setting away the remains of the loaf.

"To Gretti Jansen's, to see if she wants me to water her linen, as I used to do for play. She is lame, and it tires her to go to the spring so often. She will like me to help her, I hope; and I shall ask her for some food to pay me. Oh, I am very bold now! Soon will I beg if no other way offers." And Trudel shook her yellow head resolutely, and went to settle the stool at grandmother's feet, and to draw the curtain so that it would shield the old eyes from the summer sun.

"Heaven grant it never comes to that! It would be very hard to bear, yet perhaps we must if no help arrives. The doctor's bill, the rent, the good food thy father will soon need, will take far more than we can earn; and what will become of us, the saints only know!" answered the old woman, knitting briskly in spite of her sad forebodings.

"*I* will do it all! I don't know how, but I shall try; and, as you often say, 'Have faith and hold up thy hands; God will fill them.' "

Then Trudel went away to her work, with a stout heart under her little blue bodice; and all that summer day she trudged to and fro along the webs of linen spread in the green meadow, watering them as fast as they dried, knitting busily under a tree during the intervals.

Old Gretti was glad to have her, and at noon called her in to share the milk soup, with cherries and herrings in it, and a pot of coffee—as well as Dutch cheese, and bread full of coriander seed. Though this was a feast to Trudel, one bowl of soup and a bit of bread was all she ate; then, with a face that was not half as "bold" as she tried to make it, she asked if she might run home and take the coffee to grandmother, who longed for and needed it so much.

"Yes, indeed; there, let me fill that pewter jug with a good hot mess for the old lady, and take this also. I have little to give, but I remember how good she was to me in the winter, when my poor legs were so bad, and no one else thought of me," said

 grateful Gretti, mixing more coffee, and tucking a bit of fresh butter into half a loaf of bread with a crusty end to cover the hole.

Away ran Trudel; and when grandmother saw the "blessed coffee," as she called it, she could only sip and sigh for comfort and content, so glad was the poor old soul to taste her favorite drink again. The mother smelled it, and came down to take her share, while Trudel skipped away to go on watering the linen till sunset with a happy heart, saying to herself while she trotted and splashed:

"This day is well over, and I have kept my word. Now what *can* I do tomorrow? Gretti doesn't want me; there is no market; I must not beg yet, and I cannot finish the hose so soon.

"I know! I'll get watercresses, and sell them from door to door. They are fresh now, and people like them. Ah, thou dear duck, thank thee for reminding me of them," she cried, as she watched a mother duck lead her brood along the brook's edge, picking and dabbling among the weeds to show them where to feed.

Early next morning Trudel took her basket and went away to the meadows that lay just out of the town, where the rich folk had their summer houses, and fish ponds, and gardens. These gardens were gay now with tulips, the delight of Dutch people; for they know best how to cultivate them, and often make fortunes out of the splendid and costly flowers.

When Trudel had looked long and carefully for cresses, and found very few, she sat down to rest, weary and disappointed, on a green bank from which she could overlook a fine garden all ablaze with tulips. She admired them heartily, longed to have a bed of them for her own, and feasted her childish eyes on the brilliant colors till they were dazzled, for the long beds of purple and yellow, red and white blossoms were splendid to see, and in the midst of all a mound of dragon tulips rose like a queen's throne, scarlet, green, and gold all mingled on the ruffled leaves that waved in the wind.

Suddenly it seemed as if one of the great flowers had blown over the wall and was hopping along the path in a very curious way! In a minute, however, she saw that it was a gay parrot that had escaped, and would have flown away if its clipped wings and a broken chain on one leg had not kept it down.

32 Trudel laughed to see the bird scuttle along, jabbering to itself, and looking very mischievous and naughty as it ran away. She was just thinking she ought to stop it, when the garden gate opened, and a pretty little boy came out, calling anxiously:

"Prince! Prince! Come back, you bad bird! I never will let you off your perch again, sly rascal!"

"I will get him!" and Trudel ran down the bank after the runaway, for the lad was small and leaned upon a little crutch.

"Be careful! He will bite," called the boy.

"I'm not afraid," answered Trudel; and she stepped on the chain, which brought the "Prince of Orange" to a very undignified and sudden halt. But when she tried to catch him up by his legs, the sharp black beak gave a nip and held tightly to her arm. It hurt her much, but she did not let go, and carried her captive back to its master, who thanked her, and begged her to come in and chain up the bad bird, for he was evidently rather afraid of it.

Glad to see more of the splendid garden, Trudel did what he asked, and with a good deal of fluttering, scolding, and pecking, the Prince was again settled on his perch.

"Your arm is bleeding! Let me tie it up for you; and here is my cake to pay you for helping me. Mamma would have been very angry if Prince had been lost," said the boy, as he wet his little handkerchief in a tank of water nearby, and tied up Trudel's arm.

The tank was surrounded by pots of tulips; and on a rustic seat lay the lad's hat and a delicious large kuchen, covered with comfits and sugar. The hun-

gry girl accepted it gladly, but only nibbled at it, remembering those at home. The boy thought she did not like it, and being a generous little fellow and very grateful for her help, he looked about for something else to give her. Seeing her eyes fixed admiringly on a pretty blue and yellow pot that held a dragon tulip just ready to bloom, he said pleasantly:

"Would you like this also? All these are mine, and I can do as I like with them. Will you have it?"

"Oh, yes, with thanks! It is *so* beautiful! I longed for one, but never thought to get it," cried Trudel, receiving the pot with delight.

Then she hastened toward home to show her prize, only stopping to sell her little bunches of cresses for a few cents, with which she bought a loaf and three herrings to eat with it. The cake and the flower gave quite the air of a feast to the poor meal, but Trudel and the two women enjoyed it all, for the doctor said that father was better, and now needed only good meat and wine to grow strong and well again.

How to get these costly things no one knew, but trusted they would come, and all fell to work with lighter hearts. The mother sat again at her lacework, for now a ray of light could be allowed to fall on her pillow and bobbins by the window of the sickroom. The old woman's fingers flew as she knitted at one long blue stocking; and Trudel's little hands tugged away at the other, while she cheered her dull task by looking fondly at her dear tulip unfolding in the sun.

She began to knit next day as soon as the breakfast of dry bread and water was done; but she took her work to the doorstep and thought busily as the needles clicked, for where *could* she get money enough for meat and wine? The pretty pot stood beside her, and the tulip showed its gay leaves now, just ready to bloom. She was very proud of it, and smiled and nodded gayly when a neighbor said in passing, "A fine flower you have there."

Soon she forgot it, however, so hard was her little brain at work, and for a long time she sat with her eyes fixed on her busy hands so intently that she neither heard steps approaching, nor saw a maid and a little girl looking over the low fence at her. Suddenly some words in a strange language made her look up. The child was pointing at the tulip and talking fast in English to the maid, who shook her head and tried to lead her on.

She was a pretty little creature, all in white with a gay hat, curly locks, and a great doll in one arm, while the other held a box of bonbons. Trudel smiled when she saw the doll; and as if the friendly look decided her, the little girl ran up to the door, pointed to the flower, and asked a question in the queer tongue which Trudel could not understand. The maid followed, and said in Dutch, "Juffrouw Maud wishes the flower. Will you give it to her, child?"

"Oh, no, no! I love it. I will keep it, for now Jan is gone, it is all I have!" answered Trudel, taking the pot in her lap to guard her one treasure.

The child frowned, chattered eagerly, and offered the box of sweets, as if used to having her wishes gratified at once. But Trudel shook her head, for much as she loved "sugar drops," she loved the splendid flower better, like a true little Dutchwoman.

Then Miss Maud offered the doll, bent on having her own way. Trudel hesitated a moment, for the fine lady doll in pink silk, with a feather in her hat, and tiny shoes on her feet, was very tempting to her childish soul. But she felt that so dainty a thing was not for her, and her old wooden darling, with the staring eyes and broken nose, was dearer to her than the delicate stranger could ever be. So she smiled to soothe the disappointed child, but shook her head again.

At that, the English girl lost her temper, stamped her foot, scolded, and began to cry, ordering the maid to take the flower and come away at once.

"She *will* have it; and she must not cry. Here, child, will you sell it for this?" said the maid, pulling a handful of cents out of her deep pocket, sure that Trudel would yield now.

But the little housemother's quick eye saw that the whole handful would not buy the meat and wine, much as it looked, and for the third time she shook her yellow head. There was a longing look in her face, however; and the shrewd maid saw it, guessed that money would win the day, and diving again into her apron pocket, brought out a silver gulden and held it up.

"For this, then, little miser? It is more than the silly flower is worth; but the young lady must have all she wants, so take it and let us be done with the crying."

A struggle went on in Trudel's mind; and for a moment she did not speak. She longed to keep her dear tulip, her one joy, and it seemed so hard to let it go before she had even seen it blossom once; but then the money would do much, and her loving little heart yearned to give poor father all he needed. Just then her mother's voice came down from the open window, softly singing an old hymn to lull the sick man to sleep. That settled the matter for the dutiful daughter; tears rose to her eyes, and she found it very hard to say with a farewell caress of the blue and yellow pot as she gave it up:

"You may have it; but it *is* worth more than a gulden, for it is a dragon tulip, the finest we have. Could you give a little more? My father is very sick, and we are very poor."

The stout maid had a kind heart under her white muslin neckerchief; and while Miss Maud seized the flower, good Marta put another gulden into Trudel's hand before she hastened after her charge, who made off with her booty, as if fearing to lose it.

Trudel watched the child with the half-opened

tulip nodding over her shoulder, as though it sadly said good-bye to its former mistress, till her dim eyes could see no longer. Then she covered her face with her apron and sobbed very quietly, lest grandmother should hear and be troubled. But Trudel was a brave child, and soon the tears stopped, the blue eyes looked gladly at the money in her hand, and presently, when the fresh wind had cooled her cheeks, she went in to show her treasure and cheer up the anxious hearts with her good news.

She made light of the loss of her flower, and still knitting, went briskly off to get the meat and wine for father, and if the money held out, some coffee for grandmother, some eggs and white rolls for mother, who was weak and worn with her long nursing.

"Surely, the dear God does help me," thought the pious little maid, while she trudged back with her parcels, quite cheery again, though no pretty kitten ran to meet her, and no gay tulip stood full-blown in the noonday sun.

Still more happy was she over her small sacrifices when she saw her father sip a little of the good broth grandmother made with such care, and saw the color come into the pale cheeks of the dear mother after she had taken the eggs and fine bread, with a cup of coffee to strengthen and refresh her.

"We have enough for today, and for father tomorrow; but on Sunday we must fast as well as pray, unless the hose be done and paid for in time," said the old woman next morning, surveying their small store of food with an anxious eye.

"I will work hard, and go to Vrouw Schmidt's the minute we are done. But now I must run and get wood, else the broth will not be ready," answered Trudel, clattering on her wooden shoes in a great hurry.

"If all else fails, I too shall make my sacrifice as well as you, my heart's darling. I cannot knit as I once did, and if we are not done, or Vrouw Schmidt be away, I will sell my ring and so feed the flock till Monday," said the grandmother, lifting up one thin old hand, where shone the wedding ring she had worn so many years.

"Ah, no, not that! It was so sad to see your gold beads go, and mother's earrings and father's coat and Jan and my lovely flower! We will not sell the dear old ring. I will find a way. Something will happen, as before; so wait a little, and trust to me," cried Trudel, with her arms about her grandmother, and such a resolute nod that the rusty little black cap fell over her nose and extinguished her.

She laughed as she righted it, and went singing away, as if not a care lay heavy on her young heart. But when she came to the long dike which kept the waters of the lake from overflowing the fields below, she walked slowly to rest her tired legs, and to refresh her eyes with the blue sheet of water on one side and the still bluer flax fields on the other—for they were in full bloom, and the delicate flowers danced like fairies in the wind.

It was a lonely place, but Trudel liked it, and went on toward the wood, turning the heel of her stocking while she walked, pausing now and then to look over at the sluice gates which stood here and there ready to let off the water when autumn rains made the lake rise, or in the spring when the flax fields were overflowed before the seed was sown. At the last of these she paused to gather a bunch of yellow stonecrop growing from a niche in the strong wall which, with earth and beams, made

the dike. As she stooped, the sound of voices in the arch below came up to her distinctly. Few people came that way except little girls, like herself, to gather fagots in the wood, or truant lads to fish in the pond. Thinking the hidden speakers must be some of these boys, she knelt down behind the shrubs that grew along the banks, and listened with a smile on her lips to hear what mischief the naughty fellows were planning. But the smile soon changed to a look of terror, and she crouched low behind the bushes to catch all that was said in the echoing arch below.

"How did I think of the thing? Why, that is the best part of the joke! Mijnheer van Voost put it into my head himself," said a man's gruff voice, in answer to some question. "This is the way it was: I sat at the window of the beerhouse, and Van Voost met the burgomaster close by and said, 'My friend, I hear that the lower sluice gate needs looking to. Please see to it speedily, for an overflow now would ruin my flax fields, and cause many of my looms to stand still next winter.' 'So! It shall be looked to next week. Such a misfortune shall not befall you, my good neighbor,' said the burgomaster; and they parted. 'Aha!' thinks I to myself, 'here we have a fine way to revenge ourselves on Master van Voost, who turned us off and leaves us to starve. We have but to see that the old gate gives way *between* now and *Monday,* and that hard man will suffer in the only place where he *can* feel—his pocket.' "

Here the gruff voice broke into a low laugh, and another man said slowly:

"A good plan; but is there no danger of being found out, Peit Stensen?"

"Not a chance of it! See here, Deitrich, a quiet blow or two, at night when none can hear it, will break away these rotten boards and let the water in. The rest—it will do itself—and by morning those great fields will be many feet under water, and Van Voost's crop ruined. Yes, we *will* stop his looms for him, and other men besides you and I and Niklaas Hass will stand idle with starving children around them. Come, will you lend a hand? Niklaas is away looking for work, and Hans Dort is sick, or they might be glad to help us."

"Hans would never do it. He is sober, and so good a weaver he will never want work when he is well. I *will* be with your, Peit; but swear not to tell it, whatever happens, for you and I have bad names now, and it would go hard with us."

"I'll swear anything; but have no fear. We will not only be revenged on the master, but get the job of repairing; since men are scarce and the need will be great when the flood is discovered. See, then, how fine a plan it is! And meet me here at twelve tonight with a shovel and pick. Mine are already hidden in the wood yonder. Now, come and see where we must strike, and then slip home the other way; we must not be seen here by anyone."

There the voices stopped, and steps were heard going deeper into the arch. Trudel, pale with fear, rose to her feet, slipped off her sabots, and ran away along the dike like a startled rabbit, never pausing till she was safely around the corner and out of sight. Then she took breath, and tried to think what to do first. It was of no use to go home and tell the story there. Father was too ill to hear it or to help; and if she told the neighbors, the secret would soon be known everywhere and might bring danger on them all. No, she must go at once to

Mijnheer van Voost and tell him alone, begging him to let no one know what she had heard, but to prevent the mischief the men threatened, as if by accident. Then all would be safe, and the pretty flax fields kept from drowning. It was a long way to the "master's," as he was called, because he owned the linen factories, where all day many looms jangled, and many men and women worked busily to fill his warehouses and ships with piles of the fine white cloth, famous all the world over.

But forgetting the wood, father's broth, granny's coffee, and even the knitting which she still held, Trudel went as fast as she could toward the country house, where Mijnheer van Voost would probably be at his breakfast.

She was faint now with hunger and heat, for the day grew hot, and the anxiety she felt made her heart flutter while she hurried along the dusty road till she came to the pretty house in its gay garden, where some children were playing. Anxious not to be seen, Trudel slipped up the steps and in, at the open window of a room where she saw the master and his wife sitting at table. Both looked surprised to see a shabby, breathless little girl enter in that curious fashion; but something in her face told them that she came on an important errand, and putting down his cup, the gentleman said quickly:

"Well, girl, what is it?"

In a few words Trudel told her story, adding with a beseeching gesture, "Dear sir, please do not tell that I betrayed bad Peit and Deitrich. They know father, and may do him some harm if they discover that I told you this. We are so poor, so unhappy now, we cannot bear any more." And quite overcome with the troubles that filled her little heart, and the fatigue and hunger that weakened her little body, Trudel dropped down at Van Voost's feet as if she were dead.

When she came to herself, she was lying on a velvet sofa and the sweet-faced lady was holding wine to her lips, while Mijnheer van Voost marched up and down the room with his flowered dressing gown waving behind him, and a frown on his brow. Trudel sat up and said she was quite well; but the little white face and the hungry eyes that wandered to the breakfast table told the truth, and the good vrouw had a plate of food and a cup of warm milk before her in a moment.

"Eat, my poor child, and rest a little, while the master considers what is best to be done, and how to reward the brave little messenger who came so far to save his property," said the motherly lady, fanning Trudel, who ate heartily, hardly knowing what she ate, except that it was very delicious after so much bread and water.

In a few moments Van Voost paused before the sofa and said kindly, though his eyes were stern and his face looked hard:

"See, then, thus shall I arrange the affair, and all will be well. I will myself go to see the old gate, as if made anxious lest the burgomaster should forget his promise. I shall find it in a dangerous state, and at once set my men at work. The rascals are disappointed of both revenge and wages, and I can soon take care of them in other ways, for they are drunken fellows, and are easily clapped into prison and kept safely there till ready to work and to stop plotting mischief. No one shall know your part in it, my girl; but I do not forget it. Tell your father his loom waits for him. Meanwhile, here is something to help while he must be idle."

Trudel's plate nearly fell out of her hands as a

great gold piece dropped into her lap; and she could only stammer her thanks with tears of joy, and a mouth full of bread and butter.

"He is a kind man, but a busy one, and people call him 'hard.' *You* will not find him so hereafter, for he never forgets a favor, nor do I. Eat well, dear child, and wait till you are rested. I will get a basket of comforts for the sick man. Who else needs help at home?"

So kindly did Vrouw van Voost look and speak that Trudel told all her sad tale freely, for the master had gone at once to see the dike, after a nod and a pat on the child's head, which made her quite sure that he was not as hard as people said.

When she had opened her heart to the friendly lady, Trudel was left to rest a few moments, and lay luxuriously on the yellow sofa staring at the handsome things about her, and eating pretzels till Vrouw van Voost returned with the promised basket, out of which peeped the neck of a wine bottle, the legs of a chicken, glimpses of grapes, and many neat parcels of good things.

"My servant goes to market and will carry this for you till you are near home. Go, little Trudel;

and God bless you for saving us from a great misfortune!" said the lady; and she kissed the happy child and led her to the back door, where stood the little cart with an old man to drive the fat horse, and many baskets to be filled in town.

Such a lovely drive our Trudel had that day! No queen in a splendid chariot ever felt prouder, for all her cares were gone, gold was in her pocket, food at her feet, and friends secured to make times easier for all. No need to tell how joyfully she was welcomed at home, nor what praises she received when her secret was confided to mother and grandmother, nor what a feast was spread in the poor house that day—for patience, courage, trust in God won the battle, and the enemy had fled, and Trudel's hard siege was over.

END

LOUISA MAY ALCOTT, better known for her novels, *Little Women* and *Little Men,* left behind a treasury of stories and writings that are only now beginning to come to light.

She had early memories of "pretending to read" and "scribbling" in her father's study. A good portion of her childhood was spent entertaining the children of her famous neighbors, the Emerson's and Hawthorn's.

This feeling for making up stories and plays gradually assured her of success, when as a teacher of just sixteen, she published her first book of stories for children. Later they were published with other stories in a three-volume set called *Lulu's Library.* It is from this set that this story comes.

Besides being a noted writer, Miss Alcott was more than aware of the times she lived in. She was an early feminist who could count Miss Elizabeth Stanton as a close friend, and firmly believed in the advancement of women and little women.

STAN SKARDINSKI can remember the day his mother bought an abridged copy of *Lulu's Library* at a fair in upstate New York for ten cents. The stories inside got him through some boring times in bed with various colds.

Mr. Skardinski lives in the Park Slope section of Brooklyn, New York, known for its brownstones, in what he calls his "Victorian mobil home." If asked what he does, he will tell you he sharpens pencils a lot and sometimes finds time to draw.